TAS AND BEC 91 LIKE TO LIS' TO WORDS

KNOWLEDGE BOOKS

MASTERY DECODABLES

Gem can say words.

Gem can read words.

Tas and Bec like to listen to words in the garden.

Gem can read new words.

Gem can read new words from a book.

Gem likes to read, made and bake.

made

bake

6

Gem likes to read, pine and cone.

Gem likes to read, same and game.

pine

cone

same

game

8

Gem likes words with 'e' at the end.

Tas can listen.

Bec can listen and say the words.

Tas can not say the words.

Bec can say, made and bake, pine and cone.

Bec can say, same and game.

made

bake

pine

cone

same

game

14

Gem is happy to read words,
that end with 'e'.

Gem can read, tune, dune
and cute.

tune
dune
cute

Bec can say, tune, dune, cute.

Gem can read, late, vine, rope.

tune
dune
cute

late
vine
rope

Bec can say, late, vine, rope.

Gem, Tas and Bec like the new words that end in 'e'.